HA, HA, HA

She Was a Very Funny Girl

To Aug
and
Gavin

Enjoy, Helen T.

HELEN TSALACOPOULOS

Archway Publishing books may be ordered through booksellers or by contacting:

Archway Publishing
1663 Liberty Drive
Bloomington, IN 47403
www.archwaypublishing.com
1-(888)-242-5904

Because of the dynamic nature of the Internet, any web addresses or links contained in this book may have changed since publication and may no longer be valid. The views expressed in this work are solely those of the author and do not necessarily reflect the views of the publisher, and the publisher hereby disclaims any responsibility for them.

Certain stock imagery © Thinkstock.
Any people depicted in stock imagery provided by Thinkstock are models,
and such images are being used for illustrative purposes only.

ISBN: 978-1-4808-1319-9 (e)
ISBN: 978-1-4808-1318-2 (sc)

Printed in the United States of America.

Archway Publishing rev. date: 12/18/2014

With Love to, Anastasia & Nicole

She was a funny girl and she said very funny words. She made her friends laugh, all the time.

"Oh POOKASHEESH", she said one day as they played jumping rope games on the sidewalk.

Skip, skip, hop, hop .. don't let your pennies drop.

The word, 'POOKASHEESH' made
her friends look at each other and
then they all started to laugh.

They laughed so much that they could not turn the skipping ropes properly any more. They started to shake and dropped the skipping ropes in a jumble around their legs.

Their legs felt like they had turned to noodles and they just couldn't stand up any longer. Next, one by one, they had all fallen to the ground.

Oh no!

Ha ha, he he .. their stomachs ached, right down to their knee.

"What did you say"?, asked one of the girls.
"Did you just say, P O O K A S H E E S H?"

"Yes, you're a POOKASHEESH", said the funny girl;
as she pointed to one of her friends.

"Let's play a POOKASHEESH game", she said; as she whirled round and round with her hands up in the air.

"I like to eat POOKASHEESH", she said; as she pointed to herself and licked her lips, yum yum.

"It's just a word I like to say; it makes me smile", said the funny girl.

Well, once they all said the word out loud; they discovered that it really was a very funny word even just to say to yourself.

They all started to use the POOKASHEESH word whenever they could. It made them laugh each and every time.

Everyone who heard them say it, laughed just as much.

Soon, all the other kids at playtime, at school and their families, had now heard of the very funny word.

As the friends were playing one day; once again, the funny girl used the 'POOKASHEESH' word.

Now barely a smile appeared on their faces. The very funny word had been used so much by everyone, that now it was sounding very old to all of them.

The funny girl was not so funny anymore. Her friends really wanted to laugh like they had done before. But they were just all POOKASHEESHED out.

"Maybe we should just all go home now", said one of the friends.

They all nodded rather sadly to one another and decided that this was the end of their playtime together for the day.

"Ok, if that's what you really all want to do", said the funny girl. She shrugged her shoulders and sighed along with her friends.

Ho hum, hum ho .. no more laughing, so let's all go.

"Well, see you KURVUMPLE girls later", she said to them and waved goodbye.

"I'm going home to play with my cat, MR. GYPZOR". She smiled and winked to them all.

Giggle, giggle .. hop up and down and give your backside a wiggle.

She was still a very very funny girl; who could think of very very funny words to say, that made her friends laugh.

Some words are fun to hear or say out loud; when you just want to have fun.

Is there a funny word that *you* like to say?

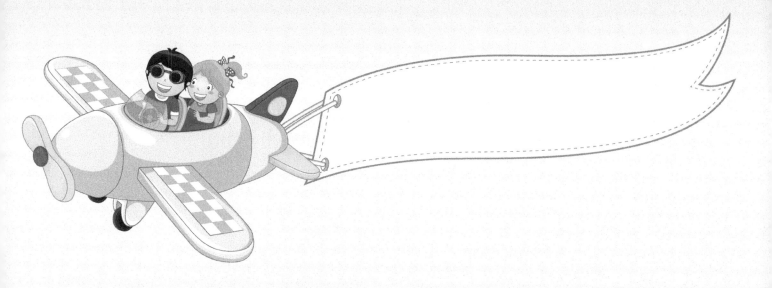

Write your funny word in the flying banner.

He, he, he .. THE END .. he, he, he